Charley's First Night

Amy Hest

illustrated by Helen Oxenbury

WALKER BOOKS
AND SUBSIDIARIES
LONDON · BOSTON · SYDNEY · AUCKLAND

It was snowing that night,

and Charley wanted me

to carry him home.

Charley's First Night

For Ken, who knows a LOT about first nights ~ A. H.

For Finn and Niamh ~ H. O.

First published 2012 by Walker Books Ltd
87 Vauxhall Walk, London SE11 5HJ

2 4 6 8 10 9 7 5 3 1

Text © 2012 Amy Hest
Illustrations © 2012 Helen Oxenbury

The right of Amy Hest and Helen Oxenbury to be identified as author and illustrator
respectively of this work has been asserted by them in accordance
with the Copyright, Designs and Patents Act 1988

This book has been typeset in Aged

Printed in China

British Library Cataloguing in Publication Data:
a catalogue record for this book is available from the British Library

ISBN 978-1-4063-3740-2

www.walker.co.uk

So I carried him all the way home.

I carried him in my old baby blanket,
which was soft and midnight blue, and we
were new together and I was very, very careful
not to slip in the snow and I thought about
his name. I was the one who thought up
his name. Charley. Charley Korn.
My name is Henry.
Henry Korn.

"This is home." That's what I told Charley when we got home, and I showed him all the rooms, including my room.

I showed him my bed and the place where my mother hides your birthday present when it's the day before your birthday. "This is home, Charley." I said that a lot so Charley would know he was home.

My mother (Mrs Korn) and my father (Mr Korn) were pretty clear about who would be in charge of walking Charley. *(I would be in charge of walking Charley, they said, and I couldn't wait to walk Charley every day for ever.)* They were pretty clear about who would be in charge of feeding Charley. *(I would be in charge of feeding Charley, they said, and I couldn't wait to feed*

Charley every day for ever.)

They were also pretty clear about where Charley would be sleeping. (*Charley would be sleeping in the kitchen, they said, and I thought about Charley in the kitchen, alone every night for ever.*)

"Charley wants to sleep in my room," I said.

"Charley will be sleeping in the kitchen," they said.

We fixed up a pillow-bed for Charley in
the kitchen, under the table where the heat
comes up, and I put my old bear, Bobo, in
the pillow-bed for Charley and I thought
about how I used to sleep with Bobo every
night. I put my small red clock between
Charley and Bobo - *tick-tock-tick-tock* -

like another little

heartbeat in

the night.

Charley curled up in a ball and I put my
face next to his and I waited for Charley
to fall asleep, and I thought about how my
mother and father sometimes used to wait for
me to fall asleep and soon Charley fell asleep.
He made a soft breathing sound and his soft
breathing sound made me sleepy, too.

I went to my room and sat up in my bed
and looked out the window and snow was
falling, over the city and the park and the
trees in the park, and I thought about
playing with Charley in the park in the snow.

The crying started in
the middle of the night
and you knew right away
it was Charley.

"Don't cry, Charley! Don't cry!" I ran to
the kitchen and scooped him and held him
close in my strong arms, and he shivered.

Slowly we walked around the house and I
showed him my room again and my bed.
I showed him my mother
and father, sound asleep
in their bed, and held
Charley close in my
strong arms.

After a while I put Charley in his pillow-bed and rubbed his tummy and Charley smiled the way a friend smiles when you say, "Hey, let's be friends for ever!" I rubbed his back and the soft place behind his ears and he was really, really sleepy and the moon made its own light that night in the kitchen, right near Charley.

"Night, Charley," I said.

"Night, Charley boy."

A long time later, I heard crying again and I flew out of bed to Charley.

"Don't cry, Charley! Don't cry!" I scooped him up and held him close in my strong arms and he shivered. I showed him how the moon made its own light in the kitchen that night. "The moon did it for you," I told Charley, and he licked my nose and it tickled.

Slowly we walked
around the house
again and I showed him
my room again. Charley
wanted me to put him on my bed, so I put
him on my bed and thought about how my
mother and father were pretty clear about
where Charley should not sleep.

Charley wanted me on my bed, so I lay down on the bed next to Charley and we looked in each other's eyes. Charley has brown eyes and mine are green and I told him we could be best friends if he wants and Charley looked in my eyes and I looked in his. "I love you, Charley boy." That's what I told Charley.

We didn't mean to fall asleep,
but we both fell asleep
on my bed . . .

and that's exactly where we slept all through
the night on Charley's first night.